Sir Handel

Based on *The Railway Series* by the Rev. W. Awdry

Illustrations by
Robin Davies and Creative Design

EGMONT

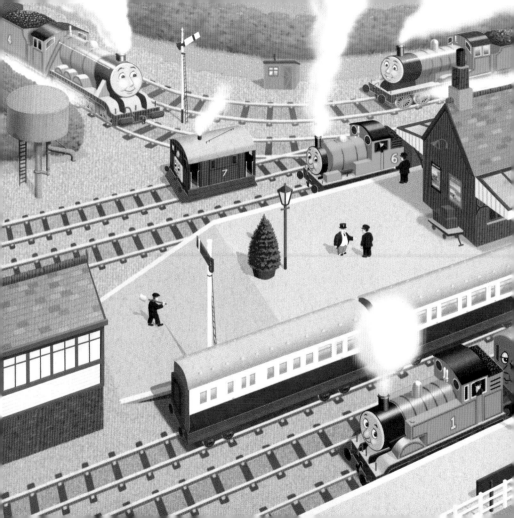

First published in Great Britain 2004
by Egmont Books Limited
239 Kensington High Street, London W8 6SA
All Rights Reserved

Thomas the Tank Engine & Friends

A BRITT ALLCROFT COMPANY PRODUCTION

Based on The Railway Series by The Rev W Awdry

© Gullane (Thomas) LLC 2004

ISBN 1 4052 1037 0
7 9 10 8
Printed in Great Britain

TO THE TRAINS ➡

This is a story about Sir Handel, who worked on the Little Railway. When he first arrived at the Little Railway, Sir Handel thought he was very important. Read this story to find out what happened when he was rude to the coaches …

Skarloey and Rheneas worked on the Little Railway. But they were growing old and tired, so The Thin Controller (who ran the Little Railway) brought two more engines to help them.

The new engines looked very smart! One was called Peter Sam and the other was called Sir Handel.

"What a small shed!" grumbled Sir Handel, when he saw his new home. "This won't do at all."

"I think it's nice," said Peter Sam.

"Humph!" replied Sir Handel. "And what's that pile of rubbish over there?"

"Shhh," replied Peter Sam. "That's Skarloey, the famous old engine!"

The next morning, the Fireman came to get Sir Handel ready for his first day's work.

"I'm tired," yawned Sir Handel. "Can Peter Sam go instead? He likes hard work – I don't know why."

"No," said the Fireman. "It's The Thin Controller's orders. You're first!"

Sir Handel's Driver arrived, and they set off to fetch the coaches.

But when Sir Handel saw them, he screeched to a standstill.

"They're not coaches!" he said. "They're so old and dirty, they look like cattle trucks!"

The five coaches – Agnes, Ruth, Lucy, Jemima and Beatrice – were very offended!

"Oooooh!" they screamed. "What a horrid engine!"

S ir Handel was coupled to the coaches, and set off towards the station. He rolled on to the platform just as Gordon arrived.

"Hello!" said Sir Handel. "Who are you?"

"I'm Gordon," said Gordon. "Who are you?"

"I'm Sir Handel. Yes, I've heard of you, Gordon. You're an Express engine, I believe. So am I, but I'm used to proper coaches – not these cattle trucks. Anyway, sorry, can't stop – must keep time, you know!"

And Sir Handel puffed off, leaving Gordon at a loss for words!

"Come along! Come along!" puffed Sir Handel to the coaches, as he pulled them along.

The coaches were very angry because Sir Handel had called them names.

"Cattle trucks! Cattle trucks!" they grumbled.

"We'll pay him back! We'll pay him back!"

Soon they came to a station. Beyond it, the line curved, then began to climb. The day was misty and the rails were slippery.

As Sir Handel prepared to set off again, Agnes had an idea.

"Hold back!" she whispered to Ruth.

"Hold back!" whispered Ruth to Lucy.

"Hold back!" whispered Lucy to Jemima.

"Hold back!" whispered Jemima to Beatrice.

The coaches giggled as Sir Handel started and their couplings tightened.

"Come on! Come on!" puffed Sir Handel as his wheels slipped on the greasy rails. He started to climb the hill, but the coaches pulled him back and the train ground to a halt.

"I can't do it! I can't do it!" Sir Handel grumbled.

"I'm used to sensible coaches, not these cattle trucks!"

The Guard came up. "I think the coaches are "up to something," he told the Driver. So they decided to bring the train down again to a level piece of line, to give Sir Handel a good start.

The Guard and the Fireman sanded the rails and Sir Handel made a tremendous effort. The coaches tried hard to drag him back, but he puffed and pulled so hard that they were soon over the hill and away on their journey.

That night, The Thin Controller spoke to Sir Handel. "You are a Troublesome Engine," he said.

"You are much too big for your wheels!"

"But those coaches were misbehaving," said Sir Handel. "They tried to stop me climbing the hill!"

"That is no surprise," said The Thin Controller, "considering how rude you were to them. You will pull trucks in the Quarry until you have learned to behave better!"

"TRUCKS?" cried Sir Handel.

Sir Handel had to shunt trucks in the Quarry for a whole week. The trucks were troublesome and would not do as they were told. He had a terrible time with them.

At the end of the week, Sir Handel was a much better behaved engine.

"Are you ready to pull coaches again?" asked The Thin Controller.

"Oh, yes please, Sir!" replied Sir Handel.

He set off to fetch his coaches and was determined to be much nicer to them.

When the coaches saw him, they muttered to each other, "Grumpy Sir Handel! Grumpy Sir Handel!" They were sure he was going to be rude again.

But Sir Handel was as polite as could be. He was coupled to the coaches and set gently off down the branch line.

And from that day on, Sir Handel tried very hard to behave. He knew he would rather pull coaches that looked like cattle trucks, than shunt real trucks in the Quarry!

The Thomas Story Library is THE definitive collection of stories about Thomas and ALL his Friends.

5 more Thomas Story Library titles will be chuffing into your local bookshop in Summer 2006:

Fergus
Mighty Mac
Harvey
Rusty
Molly

And there are even more Thomas Story Library books to follow later!
So go on, start your Thomas Story Library NOW!

A Fantastic Offer for Thomas the Tank Engine Fans!

In every Thomas Story Library book like this one, you will find a special token. Collect 6 Thomas tokens and we will send you a brilliant Thomas poster, and a double-sided bedroom door hanger! Simply tape a £1 coin in the space above, and fill out the form overleaf.

STICK
POUND
COIN
HERE

1 THOMAS TOKEN • 1 THOMAS TOKEN • 1 THOMAS TOKEN

TO BE COMPLETED BY AN ADULT

To apply for this great offer, ask an adult to complete the coupon below and send it with a pound coin and 6 tokens, to:

THOMAS OFFERS, PO BOX 715, HORSHAM RH12 5WG

☐ Please send a Thomas poster and door hanger. I enclose 6 tokens plus a £1 coin. (Price includes P&P)

Fan's name...

Address...

.... Postcode.............

Date of birth...

Name of parent/guardian.....................................

Signature of parent/guardian.................................

Please allow 28 days for delivery. Offer is only available while stocks last. We reserve the right to change the terms of this offer at any time and we offer a 14 day money back guarantee. This does not affect your statutory rights.

☐ Data Protection Act: If you do not wish to receive other similar offers from us or companies we recommend, please tick this box. Offers apply to UK only.